Louise Trapeze

CAN SO SAVE THE DAY* *really!

FACT: You won't want
to miss a single one!!!

#1 LOUISE TRAPEZE IS TOTALLY 100% FEARLESS

#2 LOUISE TRAPEZE DID NOT LOSE
THE JUGGLING CHICKENS

#3 LOUISE TRAPEZE CAN SO SAVE THE DAY

COMING SOON:
#4 LOUISE TRAPEZE WILL NOT LOSE A TOOTH

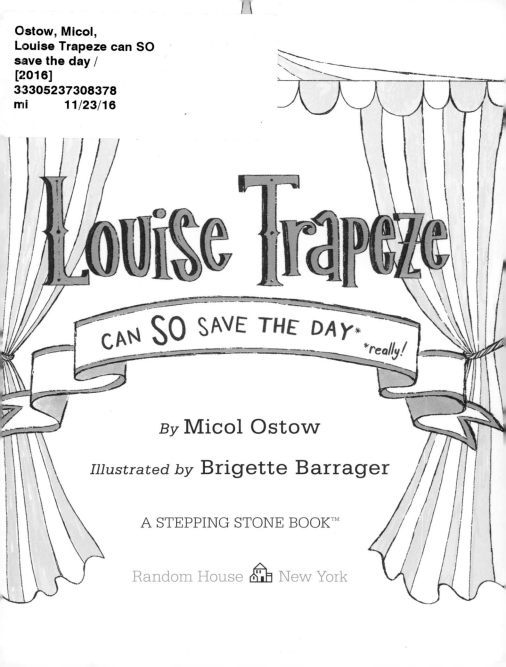

Louise Trapeze

CAN SO SAVE THE DAY* *really!

By Micol Ostow

Illustrated by Brigette Barrager

A STEPPING STONE BOOK™

Random House New York

Text copyright © 2016 by Micol Ostow
Cover art and interior illustrations copyright © 2016 by Brigette Barrager

Visit us on the Web!
SteppingStonesBooks.com
randomhousekids.com

Educators and librarians, for a variety of teaching tools,
visit us at RHTeachersLibrarians.com

Library of Congress Cataloging-in-Publication Data
Names: Ostow, Micol, author. | Barrager, Brigette, illustrator.
Title: Louise Trapeze can SO save the day / Micol Ostow ;
illustrations by Brigette Barrager.
Description: First Edition. | New York : Random House, 2016. |
"A Stepping Stone book"
Summary: The Sweet Potato Circus is in trouble, and Louise and her best friend, Stella, will do anything to save their circus—even if it means joining forces with their sworn enemy, Ferret-breath Fernando.
Identifiers: LCCN 2015035853 | ISBN 978-0-553-49750-2 (pbk.) | ISBN 978-0-553-49747-2 (hardback) | ISBN 978-0-553-49749-6 (ebook)
Subjects: | CYAC: Circus—Fiction. | Humorous stories. | BISAC: JUVENILE FICTION / Performing Arts / Circus. | JUVENILE FICTION / Humorous Stories. | JUVENILE FICTION / Readers / Chapter Books.
Classification: LCC PZ7.O8475 Lj 2016 | DDC [Fic]—dc23

MANUFACTURED IN CHINA
10 9 8 7 6 5 4 3 2 1

This book has been officially leveled by using the
F&P Text Level Gradient™ Leveling System.

✳ CONTENTS ✳

1

COTTON CANDY CRAZY!

"*Olé!*" Ringmaster Riley boomed from the back of the circus ring.

"*Olé!*" the crowd shouted back, clapping their hands like wildness.

(*Olé* is Spanish for *hooray for Louise!*)

Oona the Juggling Chicken and I had just finished our newest routine: the Tightwire Tango. We did a whole tightwire walk with *amazing fancy jumps* set to special Spanish tango music! Can you *even*?

Our performance was *superb*. We even leaped from the tightwire onto Clementine the Elephant's back! Then Clem waved her trunk at the crowd. The audience stomped their feet so hard I thought they would stomp right through the ground!

(Crowds *love* when Clementine waves.)

Bright, circusy music started up. I waved, and Oona flapped her wing. Tolstoy the Clown led us out of the ring and through the Big Top doorway.

"We did it!" I shouted once we were outside.

"You sure did!" Tolstoy said. His big red clown-makeup mouth was turned up in a *giant* smile. He lifted me (and Oona) down to the ground.

"Great job, guys," Stella said. She was waiting for me right outside the tent.

Stella Dee Saxophone is my BFF best friend. She and her parents, Max Saxophone and Ms. Minnie Dee, are *actually* Clementine's trainers. They perform with Clem every night. But sometimes they let me do *unique* tricks with her for special occasions! Like tonight!

"I'll take Clem to Max and Minnie for some water," Tolstoy said. "Can you guys take Oona back to Chuck Cluck?"

"Of course!" Stella and I said together.

Chuck Cluck was in our "backstage" tent. Stella and I started to walk over there. But the closer we got to the tent, the flappier Oona went with her wings.

And then! Completely from nowhere! Out leaped a giant jumping whirl of a person—and a whiskery *ferret*.

Ferret-breath Fernando! Fernando was Ringmaster Riley's son and my big-time enemy. Of *course* he was the one jumping out at Stella and me. He is such a gooberhead.

"Ack!" I shouted. "Fernando! Why are you sneaking up on Stella and me?" For once, he wasn't wearing his

stilts, so I could stare right into his beady, gooberish eyes.

Fernando snickered. "Scared you, didn't I?" he asked.

Fernando likes to tease me because I am only ninety-eight percent fearless. Ninety-eight is a lot of percents! But it's not *all* of them. (One hundred is all of them.) He thinks he is braver than Stella and me because he is nine whole years old, and Stella and I are still only seven. *Pfft.*

"You *startled* me," I said. *Startled* is not exactly the same as being scared—more like a scaredish surprise.

Fernando rolled his eyes. "Fine. I startled you." He laughed again. Then he lowered his voice to a whisper. "But do you want to see something for-real scary?"

Stella's eyes went wide-wide-wide. She didn't look too sure. "Maybe," she said. (Stella is not one hundred percent fearless, either!)

"Look," Fernando said. He pointed past the back-stage tent. "Over there. My dad is *arguing* with Ethel Teitelbaum!"

I gasped. *Arguing* means people are having a problem! That was for-real scary. We Sweet Potatoes do not argue very much, thank goodness gracious.

Stella and I looked where Fernando was pointing. Right away, I could see Ethel Teitelbaum, our Refreshments Queen, looking upset. Next to her was her big, shiny cotton candy machine.

And that machine was the reason she was upset!

The cotton candy machine was going totally berserker! Huge, puffy clouds of pink and blue cotton candy were exploding everywhere, covering the machine. There were giant globs of Easter-egg-colored cotton candy on the ground! And behind Ethel, I could see some audience members with sticky, cotton-candy-crazy chins and cheeks. One little girl even had a huge swirl of cotton candy on her head like a bird's nest!

It looked very delicious, to be one hundred percent honest. But also, it definitely looked like a problem!

"What happened?" Stella asked.

"Dad is upset about the broken cotton candy machine," Fernando explained. "Some of the audience members are angry because they got covered in cotton candy when it exploded. And some are complaining because they couldn't have cotton candy after Ethel had to shut the machine down!"

"Yikes!" I said. Oona gave a worried-ish cluck from my shoulder. Complaining was not good at all! We wanted to keep our circus audience one hundred percent happy, one hundred percent of the time!

"*Yikes* is right," Fernando agreed. "Too many complaints could be bad news for the Sweet Potatoes. We might even have to *close the show*!"

Stella's eyes went watery. "Fernando, we don't believe you!" she said. "You're just *overreacting*."*

Overreacting = making a giant, stinky deal about something that's not a big deal at all. Like the time Mama got upset with me for painting my costume shoes sparkly purple. That purple was the prettiest!

(Also, it washed right off.)

"Believe what you want," Fernando said. "You'll see."

"Ugh, don't listen to him, Stella," I said. "Whatever happened with the cotton candy machine, it was definitely an *accident*. I'm sure it's not a for-serious argument." I said it in my loudest voice, to help make myself believe it.

Still, though . . . it was an awful lot of cotton candy puffing and spilling all over the place! The bird's-nest girl was pulling chunks of cotton candy off her head and gulping it down.

"You're probably right," Stella said hopefully.

"Why don't you go catch up to your parents and Clem?" I said. "I'll take Oona back to Chuck Cluck. It's almost time for the finale."

Stella agreed, and we both walked off. (We gave Fernando stinky looks before we walked away.)

It didn't take long to get to Chuck Cluck. But right at the very outside of the backstage tent, I heard grown-up voices.

The voices were whispery.

And those whispery voices sounded worried!

Uh-oh! I had to listen in and find out why. . . .

2

WHISPERY THINGS

I stopped right outside the backstage tent. I wanted to hear the grown-up whispering! But I couldn't understand anything from so far away.

I turned to Oona. "Do you hear that?"

She nodded.

"What do you think it is?" I asked.

She did a chickeny kind of shrug at me like she had no worldwide idea.

Quiet as mice, Oona and I peeked our heads

through the tent flap. There was Chuck Cluck. Loona and Maude were with him, in a small wire cage. Next to Chuck was Cady the Bearded Lady. I couldn't see their faces, but they were standing in a very serious-business way. Their voices were still low and whis-pery. That meant they had an important grown-up secret.

I *craned** my neck so my head was stretched as far out and close to them as it could go.

⭑ Craned = pushed and twisted and made very extremely long

Finally, I could hear the littlest bit of grown-up talking.

And it did *not* sound good.

Tiny pieces of words floated at me. I tried to under-stand them as best I could. It sounded like Cady was talking. All I could hear were *"audience"* and *"sales DOWN."*

Uh-oh. This was *definitely* not good. *DOWN* meant we were selling *fewer* tickets than usual! Maybe not enough tickets at all.

Was this all because of the cotton candy craziness? Was Fernando *right*? If people were complaining and sales were down, would we have to close the whole entire circus?

More words floated by. *"Save . . . performance."*

Save the performance?

I was trying hard to be sneaky, but I couldn't help it: I let out a big-time gasp.

Right away, Chuck Cluck and Cady turned around. Chuck smiled extra big, like he was super happy to see me. But I knew better! I'd heard all those whispery words, after all.

"Louise!" he cried. "How was the new act?"

Well, if Chuck was pretending to be happy and regular, then I would pretend, too. I made my face extra smile-ish, just like his.

"Superb!" I said. "Oona stayed perfectly balanced,

and we did a jumping spin right onto Clementine's back. It was amazing."

(It's not braggy to call something amazing if it's the truth.)

"I'm sure it was!" he said. He still sounded the cheeriest.

FACT: Sometimes grown-ups do not want kids to know their worry-ish thoughts. They like to pretend everything is fine-fine-fine. It's so ANNOYING!

But I had heard the whispering with my very own ears! And I saw Ethel Teitelbaum and Ringmaster Riley having an argument, too. And that berserker cotton candy machine. So I knew there was a problem. No matter how much Chuck and Cady smiled at me.

"Thanks for taking such good care of Oona," Chuck said. "I know she felt special being part of your show."

"She's the specialest!" I agreed.

It was the truth. *Everyone* in our circus troupe was super-extremely special! So if there was a problem?

I, Louise Trapeze, would have to solve it!

3

AN EMERGENCY PROBLEM!

Mama and Daddy will definitely know the whole story, I thought. I would find them and ask!

I said goodbye to Chuck, Cady, and the chickens and went back to the Big Top tent. Right outside, Tolstoy the Clown was juggling away.

But I didn't know *why* he was juggling. The show was almost over, after all. Maybe he just wanted some extra practice? Except, right now he was juggling *very* quickly! *Much* more quickly than normal times. Those juggling balls were whirling around and around! Tolstoy looked like he was performing his act in real-life fast-forward! It was the strangest.

Tolstoy did a quick *hello* nod. I was still confused, but I just nodded back. I was in an extra hurry, too—I needed to talk to Mama and Daddy right away, before we all had to go out for our big *finale*!

I found them both a little bit closer to the Big Top tent flap, doing their stretches for their *curtain call.**

✸ CURTAIN CALL= a final bow at the end of a big-time performance.
It's my one hundred percent favorite part of the show because we get to bow and twirl, and the crowd claps extra loud!!!

"Great job tonight, Lou!" Mama called when she saw me. Her leg was pulled all the way straight up against her so she looked like the letter *I*.

(Mama is super bendy!)

"Thanks!" I said. "But we need to talk!" I did a serious face. "I think there is a *Sweet Potato Emergency Problem*!"

"Really?" Mama lowered her leg back onto the ground so we were both standing like regular people again. She crouched down next to me. "What is it?"

Now I was the one with a whispery voice. "First, Ringmaster Riley was arguing with Ethel Teitelbaum about the broken cotton candy machine. And then! I heard Chuck Cluck talking to Cady the Bearded Lady. He said ticket sales are *down*."

Mama looked at me. Her eyebrows were pointy like she was maybe not-believing me.

I tapped my foot in an impatient way. "And *down* is the opposite of *up*."

Mama smiled. "That's true."

"This is not a time for smiling!" I said. My voice was a little bit shouty. "If we don't sell enough

tickets, the Sweet Potato Circus might have to close! And then what?"

It was time to tell Mama everything I'd heard. "Cady said we need to *save the circus*! I heard it with my own two ears. And you only save things that are *in trouble*!"

Mama leaned close-close-close to me and wrapped me in a hug. "I can see why you're upset," she said. "It would be sad if the circus had to close."

"It would be the saddest *ever*!" I agreed.

"But that's not going to happen," Mama said. "You must have heard wrong. If the circus needed saving, don't you think Daddy and I would know about it?"

I shrugged. Mama had a point, but I was still worried!

"But Cady said—" I started.

Mama interrupted me. (Interrupting is mostly rude,

but sometimes adults are allowed to do it when they think children are getting *carried away*.)

"Lou, what have Daddy and I told you about *eavesdropping*?"* she asked.

*Eavesdropping= listening in on other people's whispering conversations. It's like snooping, and almost as rude as interrupting.

I frowned. "Not to do it."

"Exactly." She raised her eyebrows again so they were *very* pointy. "Now, I don't know what you heard, but I *do* know you probably misunderstood. You have nothing to worry about. The Sweet Potato Circus is going to be around for a long, long time."

"Really?" I asked.

"Really," Mama replied. She pointed to where Tolstoy was still whoosh-whoosh-*whoosh*ing his juggling balls around lickety-split quick. "Who wouldn't buy a ticket to see that?"

Now Mama *really* had a point. "Okay," I said. "If you promise."

I was still an eensy bit worried. But Mama seemed completely sure everything was fine. And she was a grown-up. That meant she knew things.

"I purple pony promise." Mama took my hand. "So are you ready for our curtain call?"

I nodded and tried to push the worrying thoughts away. For now, it was time to take a bow!

4

BEING NOT-BELIEVED

The next morning, my BFF, Stella, and I were doing math problems in our classroom trailer. But I could *not* concentrate. All I could think about was what Cady had said about saving the performance.

If the Sweet Potato Circus closed, I wouldn't get to do any more *superb* tricks on the flying trapeze. And I wouldn't get to do any more curtain calls, either.

And if the circus closed, there would be no more special circus class! And circus class is *so much fun!*

Instead of regular school, Stella, Fernando, and I have a tutor who travels with our troupe and teaches us. Our tutor's name is Jed, and he is extremely good at keeping us smart. Jed is a grown-up who did college and everything. He doesn't perform in our circus, but he's very strong. He lifts weights every morning outside his trailer. He also rides a *dirt bike,* which is an extra-speedy bicycle that has an *engine*! It is loud-loud-loud (in a good way!).

So Stella and I were doing math and Fernando was reading. Linus, Fernando's pet ferret, was batting an eraser all around.

FACT: Another fun thing about circus class is that you're allowed to bring pets, like ferrets. I've never been to regular school, but I bet they don't let you have ferrets there!!!

But instead of thinking about school, I was busy worrying. How could I convince Mama that we had a real-live emergency problem?

"In this next math problem, there is a movie theater with ten seats," Jed said. "Four people have bought movie tickets. So how many more tickets does the theater need to sell in order to fill up all its seats?"

Tickets? Seats? This math word problem was exactly the same as the *actual* Sweet Potato problem going around and around in my brain! In real life, we didn't sell enough tickets to fill all our Big Top seats. That's what Cady the Bearded Lady said.

"Louise, you seem *distracted** today," Jed said.

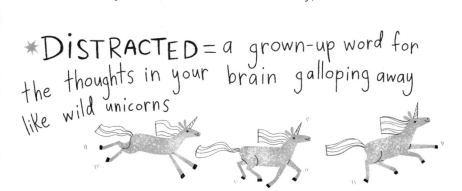

*DISTRACTED = a grown-up word for the thoughts in your brain galloping away like wild unicorns

I sighed. "I am."

"What is it?" Stella asked.

"Well . . . ," I said, "Mama says it's nothing. . . ."

"Hmm," Jed said. "If your mother says it's nothing, I'm sure you can trust her."

"Even if the circus is going to *close*?" I asked.

It was out! I didn't mean for my inside thoughts to explode and make everyone worried. But I couldn't help it.

Stella gasped. Even Fernando couldn't hide his surprise-y face.

Jed just looked very confused. "What makes you think the circus is going to close, Louise?" he asked.

I swallowed. "First, we all saw Ethel Teitelbaum and Ringmaster Riley having an argument when the cotton candy machine went crazy," I said. Fernando and Stella nodded at that.

"It's true," Fernando said. "My dad said some people were complaining about the broken machine, too."

"But then! I also heard Chuck Cluck talking last night. He told Cady the Bearded Lady that ticket sales are *down*. Down! Like that movie theater in the word problem with all those empty seats! What will happen if we don't sell enough tickets?"

"Oh no!" Stella cried.

But Jed's forehead unwrinkled. He didn't look confused anymore. Now he just had a grown-up, smarter-than-you face on.

"Your mother was right, Louise," he said. "You probably misunderstood what you heard."

"I *didn't* misunderstand!" I scrunched my nose up in my angriest way. Why were grown-ups always so busy not-believing what kids say? Even about things we heard with our very own earholes!

Being not-believed is the *worst*.

"Ticket sales are not for you kids to worry about,

Louise," Jed said. "Or adult arguments, either. The cotton candy machine can be fixed. Everything is just fine with the circus."

I didn't *totally* believe him, even though I wanted to. But just then there was a knock at the trailer door. It was Petrova the Human Pretzel. She had a message for Jed from Ringmaster Riley.

"I'll be right back," Jed said. He moved toward the doorway. "Fernando, keep reading. Louise and Stella, solve the word problem and show me your work. And *all* of you— *calm down.*"

But those unicorns were still galloping away in my brain. As soon as the trailer door closed behind Jed, I turned to Fernando and Stella.

"I don't care if Jed says not to worry," I said to them. "If ticket sales are down, that is *extremely bad news.*"

"I agree," Stella said.

Fernando sighed. "I agree, too," he said at last. Linus swished his tail to say so did he.

My mouth dropped open, I was so surprised.

Fact: Fernando never <u>agrees</u> with Stella and me. He says we <u>are</u> too <u>babyish</u>. If Fernando agreed with two seven-year-olds, then this <u>really</u> was serious business!

"This is an *emergency problem,*" I said in my most dramatic voice. Fernando and Stella both nodded. "It's up to us to save the day!"

"But how?" Stella asked.

"Lucky for us, I have a *eureka!* idea," I said. I leaned

closer to them. "We need to come up with an *amazing* new act for our show!"

"Perfectamundo!" Stella said. "Then people will buy more tickets and—"

"—the circus will be saved!" Fernando interrupted.

It was extremely rude of him to interrupt, but I didn't care. For once, Fernando was totally and completely right!

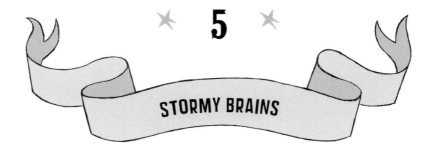

5

STORMY BRAINS

Stella, Fernando, and I agreed to work together to think up new acts for the circus. In class when we have to think very hard, it's sometimes called *brainstorming*. Brainstorming works better when you have lots of people cooperating to think.

FACT: I'm excellent at cooperating. EXCEPT for once when Fernando and I were supposed to glue a model butterfly chrysalis in class for Jed. But actually, Fernando is a glue stick hogger. So that time was not my fault.

We planned to meet behind the Big Top tent after siesta. Most of the grown-ups were drinking coffee and doing errandy things then, so we knew no one would ask what we were up to. I had a stripy bag filled with lots of props we could use for trying out tricks. It was time to get our brains all stormy!

It was very quiet while I walked to our meeting spot. But I did see one strange-ish thing:

Just beside the box office tent, our Fire-Eater, El Fuego Mateo, was practicing swallowing giant torches of flameyness!

Now, Mateo *always* gobbles down fire the way normal people eat ice cream and other regular food things. But today he was gulping those flames away at super-high speed! It was just like how Tolstoy was juggling in fast-forward yesterday.

Why were all the Sweet Potatoes suddenly moving so lickety-split quick?

I didn't have time to ask, though. I could see that Stella was already down by the Big Top with Clementine. Fernando was right next to her, high-high-high up on his stilts. When I saw them, I forgot all about Mateo.

"I hope you've both been thinking hard about your acts," I said. "It's time to *storm*! With our *brains*! Because we might be the Sweet Potatoes' *only hope*."*

★ ONLY HOPE = the only ones who can save the whole entire day!

"Well, I'm a great brainstormer," Fernando said. "My idea will probably be the best." He made a smirk.

(Ooh, he was even a know-it-all when he was cooperating!)

"We'll see about that!" Stella said. She looked at me. "Can I go first? Prettiest please?"

"Of course you can," I told her. "We need to make the ideas *storm from our brains*," I said. "Everyone, think of things Stella can do in her act."

"She stands on Clementine," Fernando said.

"That is true," I agreed. "But think stormier! What can she do *while she is standing on Clementine* that would be more special?"

Stella tapped her chin with her finger. "Hmm."

"Hmm," I said.

Fernando wrinkled his forehead like he was thinking, too. "Hmm."

Stella looked at me. I knew what she was thinking: this brainstorming was not nearly stormy enough. "What do you have in that bag, Lou?" she asked. "Maybe there's a prop that will give us an idea."

"I'm glad you asked," I said. I opened 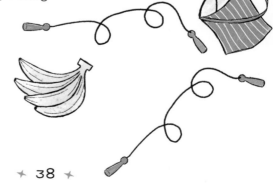 the bag and pulled things  out: a silver horn with a shiny red squeaker, three jump ropes, a wig made of glittery gold tinsel. . . .

"Ooh!" I said, pulling out one more thing. "It's a bunch of bananas!"

Stella's eyebrows went up-up-up. We both had the same idea about those bananas! I broke off three of them for Stella.

I stepped forward and made a trumpet sound. "Presenting . . . Stella Dee Saxophone and Clementine the Elephant!" I called. "Starring in—" I looked at Stella. "What should we call this trick?"

Stella shrugged. "I don't know! We just thought of it," she said.

"Starring in *Something Superb That Will Have a Real Name Later!*" I shouted.

Clementine wrapped her trunk around Stella and lifted her onto her back. Stella unbunched the bananas and raised them one at a time, like she was showing them off to an imaginary audience.

"Ladies and gentlemen, I will now *juggle these three bananas* while standing on tiptoe on Clementine's back!" Stella announced. She pointed her toes so she was the tallest she could be.

Zip-zap-zip! Stella tossed the bananas high into the air. I held my breath, waiting to see her juggle.

I waited a few seconds more.

Those bananas sure were high up.

Even Stella looked surprised at how high they went. She tilted her neck to look at them. But I guess the sun got in her eyes, because she blinked.

Boom! Bang! Bop!

One banana landed on the ground. One bounced right off Fernando's head!

Stella reached to grab the last one, but it slipped past her fingers. Clementine stretched out her trunk and caught it. Then she *ate it* in one huge gulp!

"Whoops," Stella said sadly.

"You just need to practice some more," I told her. "Practice makes perfect!"

(That's what Mama always says.)

"Maybe," Stella said. "But even if I do, it probably isn't a stormy enough trick. We already have juggling *chickens* in our circus! And Tolstoy juggles, too. So maybe another juggler isn't *actually* that special."

"You may have a point," I said. I sighed.

But Stella didn't stay sad. She turned to Fernando. "Now it's *your* turn. What should *your* act be?"

"Something on stilts," Fernando said.

"Well, of course!" I agreed. Fernando does almost everything on stilts. He would probably sleep in them, if his bed weren't too short.

Thinking about Fernando lying down in stilts gave me an idea. "It's too bad you can't do a cartwheel on

stilts," I said. Cartwheels are fun, and a stilt cartwheel would be the highest cartwheel of ever!

Fernando frowned. "That would be exciting. But I don't think I can learn a cartwheel in time for our next show."

Stella was making a brainstormy face again. "Can you . . . *jump* on your stilts?" she asked.

Fernando gave her a look. "Of course." He glanced around. "But what can I jump over?"

Now *my* brain was storming! I grabbed two jump ropes. "I know!"

I set up the jump ropes wide-wide-wide apart in the grass, like there was a river between them. If this trick worked, it would for sure be extra special. The only time I ever saw jump ropes in the Sweet Potato Circus was with Stefano Wondrous's Wonder Dogs. And sometimes Tolstoy the Clown. But none of them ever used stilts at the same time.

FACT: The Wonder Dogs are excellent jump ropers. Better than Tolstoy, even!

"So . . . I jump across the jump ropes?" Fernando asked.

I nodded. "We'll call this trick *Jump the River*!"

"Okay," Fernando said. He turned to Linus, who was resting on his shoulder. "Why don't you wait on the ground for this?" he asked. "I need to balance."

Once Linus was settled, Fernando walked backward on his stilts until he was a few whole Louise lengths away from the jump ropes. He took a big breath, then counted quietly to himself.

"One, two . . . *three!*"

On *three*, Fernando went running faster than ever, right toward the jump ropes. *"Geronimo!"* he shouted.

Just before he got to the first jump rope, he pressed as hard as he could into the ground with his stilts. *Ka-boing!* Up into the air Fernando went!

But—oh no! As he sailed forward, Fernando's right stilt got all tangled up with his left stilt!

"Ack!" Fernando called. He started wobbling all over. It looked like he was going to *ka-boom!* straight down onto the ground.

Thank goodness gracious, Clementine knew just what to do. She reached out her trunk to help catch Fernando!

"Are you okay?" I asked. Fernando might be my number one enemy a lot of the time, but I didn't want him to get hurt!

He shrugged. "I'm fine," he said. But his voice was

gruffish. He didn't look so happy about
being caught by an elephant.

"I messed up my trick, too," Stella
reminded him. "Everyone messes up
sometimes."

"Even nine-year-olds," I added. I smiled so Fernando would know I was teasing.

"Okay, okay," Fernando said. He waved his hand, but I could tell he was getting less grumpy. "Last but not least . . ." He waggled an eyebrow at me.

"Last but not least!" I agreed.

It was time for my very own one hundred percent stupendous act!

6

LAST BUT NOT LEAST

Fact: The Sweet Potato Circus's ticket sales were *down.*

Fact: Fernando, Stella, and I had to come up with a *stupendous* new act to get people to come to our show and buy tickets!

Fact: Neither of our brainstorms for Stella's and Fernando's new acts had worked out at all.

That meant it was time for me to *pull out all the stops.**

Pull out all the stops = do your very best job ever in order to <u>save the day</u>!

I was an eensy bit nervous about being the Sweet Potatoes' very last hope. But I had no choice!

"Let's brainstorm for *you*, Lou," Stella said.

"Actually," I replied, "when we were doing Fernando, I had a brilliant *eureka!* idea all on my own!"

(Sometimes that happens with brainstorming.)

Quickly, I led everyone to my tightwire. It was a little lower than a real-live grown-up tightwire. Low down enough that I didn't need a net.

But it was still a little bit scary!

I took a deep being-fearless breath and scampered to the top of the tightwire. Everyone watched me extra closely. Stella, Fernando, and even Clementine and Linus had their eyeballs trained right on me!

I felt the peanut-butter-lumpish kind of nervous in my throat.

Don't worry, I told myself. *You, Louise Trapeze, are ninety-eight percent fearless.* That was a lot of percents! And I'd done the tightwire zillions of times, even if I'd never done this exact trick before.

It was time. *Tip-tap-toe.* I inched along the wire, ballerina-graceful.

Zip-zap-zip! I sprang up in a dancer twirl and turned all the way around. Stella clapped her hands very excitedly.

But that wasn't even the special trick! That was just the beginning!

I put one leg in front of the other on the wire and stretched my hands into the air.

Spring-sprang-sproing! I leaped forward, grabbing the wire with my right hand, and then my left. I made my muscles extra tight and sent my legs up-up-up.

Fliiiip!

Flop!

Oops!

What I meant to
do: a *stupendous*
cartwheel on top
of the tightwire.

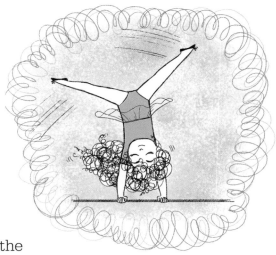

What I *actually* did:
a *gigantic* belly flop off the

tightwire

and onto the grass!

"Louise! Are you
okay?" Suddenly,
Stella's face was
right next to mine.

I pushed myself

up and looked back at her. "I think so." I sat extremely

still for a minute, to see how my arms and legs were

feeling. They were fine. The only problemy thing was my stomach: it was squeezing from belly-flop embarrassment!

Even Fernando had come down off his stilts to see if I was all right. "How many fingers is this?" he asked. He held up two fingers like bunny ears.

"Two," I said. "Of course."

Fernando shrugged. "I saw that on TV once. If you can tell how many fingers, it means your brains are okay."

That was good to hear. But my brains weren't *totally* okay. They were still very worried!

"But our brainstorming didn't work!" I cried. "We didn't come up with a new act! How are we going to save the Sweet Potatoes now?"

No one answered me. No one had any *eureka!* ideas at all.

I sighed.

Stella sighed.

Even Clementine sighed, in an elephantish way.

But Fernando wasn't sighing. Instead, he was completely distracted!

I stomped my foot. "Fernando!" I called. "What are you looking at? We are not finished cooperating!"

I glanced over to where he was staring. Off in the field, Jed was on his dirt bike. The engine was revving like a tiger, and he was turning very tilty circles so the bike dipped low-low-low on its side.

It was *extremely* exciting to watch, actually. I could see why Fernando was so distracted.

Zoom-zoom-zoom! Jed raced his dirt bike up the field toward us *just on his back wheel*! Clouds of dust exploded from his bike wheels. I never saw anything like it!

Vroom! Jed slid his bike to a stop a few feet in front of us (far enough away for safety, of course).

"Whoa," Fernando said. "Can you teach me to ride like that?" His eyes were as big as the dinner plates Stella's mama sometimes spins in her act.

"When you're bigger, sure," Jed said. "What are you troublemakers up to?"

No one said anything. We didn't want Jed to know we were brainstorming ways to save the circus. Not after he told us to calm down. We weren't being calm at all!

"Never mind," Jed decided. "I don't want to know. As long as you're ready for class tomorrow. Lou, Stella—I've got new word problems for you!"

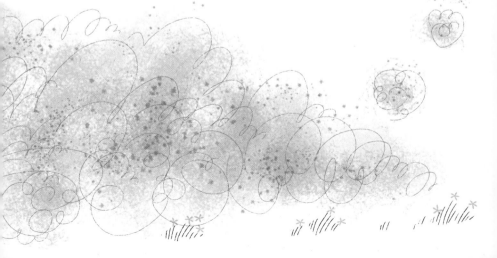

Stella and I made polite smiles. We waved at Jed and promised we'd be ready. He waved back and zoomed away again—safely, of course.

Right away when he was gone, I stopped smiling. Word problems, real-live Sweet Potato Emergency problems . . .

With so many problems, how would I *ever* save the day?

7

FUNNY MONEY

Jed was not joking about giving us more word problems. The next day, we had to solve special ones about money! Jed likes to call math problems with dollars and cents "funny money" problems.

Fact: Math with money is much fancier than just-plain math with regular numbers.

"An ice-cream cone costs one dollar," Jed said. "But, Louise, you have two quarters, and Stella also has two quarters."

A quarter is only twenty-five cents. And a dollar is one hundred whole cents! So fifty cents was not nearly enough cents for an ice-cream cone, actually.

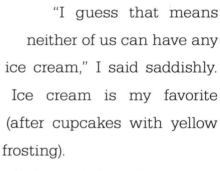

"I guess that means neither of us can have any ice cream," I said saddishly. Ice cream is my favorite (after cupcakes with yellow frosting).

Jed smiled. "That's one way to look at the problem. But it doesn't sound like a very cheerful solution, does it?"

"No," Stella said. "It doesn't sound cheerful at all." (Stella likes ice cream even more than I do!)

"Well, let's get creative in our thinking," Jed said. "How many quarters are there in a dollar?"

"That's easy," Fernando snickered. "Four."

"Correct," Jed replied. "But you're supposed to be reading."

Fernando rolled his eyes and picked his book back up.

I went to make a face at Fernando. But then—I had an eensy-weensy *eureka!* thought. And *actually,* it came from Fernando butting his big old nose into our funny money math. *Butting in* is rude. But it made me think about cooperation and working together.

"Oh!" I jumped up from my seat. "What if Stella and I put our money together? Then we could buy one ice-cream cone and share it!"

"Eureka!" Stella shouted.

"Perfect! That's exactly how I hoped you'd solve this

problem. With teamwork!"
Jed said. "Although, next
time do you think you
could wait to be called
on, instead of yelling
out the answer?" Jed
smiled, so I knew he
wasn't really upset with me.

"Sure!" I agreed.

I was extra proud of myself for solving the funny
money problem. But also, I was thinking my very
hardest about the Sweet Potato Emergency Problem.

Brainstorming together was not enough to come up
with a stupendous new act for the circus. Brainstorming was a kind of *thinking* together.

But maybe Stella, Fernando, and I needed to be
working together!

I finally knew just how to save the Sweet Potato Circus!

Instead of just brainstorming acts for *each other,* Fernando, Stella, and I needed to come up with one extra-ultra-stupendous *teamwork* act!

That was definitely for sure going to work. It just had to!

Teamwork was completely the way to save the whole entire day!

8

THREE HEADS ARE BEST

"**W**hat we need to do is to think of things *all three of us* are excellent at," I said. "Tricks we can do *together* to make one new act. Instead of just brainstorming different ideas for each other separately. *Teamwork* will save the circus."

Stella and Fernando and I were behind the Easy Trapezee tent while the rest of the Sweet Potatoes were siesta-ing. (*Siesta* is a fancy word for *rest*.) Clementine and Linus were keeping us company. We were thinking our hardest to come up with ideas. Even with three heads doing three times the thinking, it was still taking a whole bunch of minutes to come up with a different, *eureka!*-amazing act. But that's how good ideas work.

Fact: If eureka! amazing ideas were easy to come up with, they wouldn't be good enough to save the whole entire day!

"We could maybe juggle something special," Stella suggested. "Like juggling all together, I mean."

"Except," Fernando said, "when you were juggling the bananas, you dropped them."

Stella frowned, but Fernando was just telling the truth. "You're right," she said.

"We could have a ferret race," Fernando said. He held out his arm so Linus could scamper across it like a jungle gym.

"But we only have one ferret. And besides, Linus is not super fast," I said. I pointed at Linus. His scampering was medium-quick. Also he kept slipping to one side of Fernando's arm.

Suddenly, I sat up straight-straight-straight. "That's it!" I cried. *"Balance!"*

Stella and Fernando stared right at me. Of course, they didn't understand my brilliantness yet.

"All three of us are completely excellent at balance," I explained. "I balance on my tightwire, Stella balances on top of Clementine, and, Fernando, you balance on your stilts. So our new act should be something about *balancing.*"

Now Stella understood. "Good idea, Louise!" she shouted. She jumped up. "Oh! Do you know what would make our balancing act even more special? Stefano Wondrous's Wonder Dogs!"

"Stella!" I shouted. "That idea is *perfectamundo!*

Especially because there are *three* wonder dogs, and there are *three* of us!"

FACT: I am excellent at math and numbers!

9 11 ÷ 4 128
2 5 7 = 8
0 × 6 + 10
3

Stella giggled, and Clementine trumpeted to say she agreed this was a great plan. Even Fernando was excited. His face was very smile-ish.

"I know you're a little bit afraid of heights, Louise," he said. "But maybe we could do something with a flip off Clementine and onto your trampoline? That's pretty special. Could you try it?"

I couldn't believe it—for once, Fernando was asking me a for-serious question, not teasing me.

I thought very extremely hard. "That's a good idea! Stella and I could ride out on Clem with the dogs

balanced behind us on
her back. I could flip from
Clementine onto my tram-
poline. Then the dogs
could jump from Clem

to me, and then—*bounce!*—up in the air again to
balance on *your* arms and head while you're on your
stilts."

It was a lot of bouncing. And a *lot* of balancing. But
I knew if I could just be one hundred percent brave,
we could do it!

"Yes!" Fernando said. "Then you could backflip on your trampoline while Stella backflips on top of Clementine!"

"And then! Clem could pick you up again with her trunk," Stella said. "Fernando could stilt-walk closer to us. Then two of the dogs could jump from him to us, Lou! Each one of us would balance one dog!"

I knew teamwork was going to solve our problem! This act would for sure save the circus! "Yes! And then we could do a parade out of the ring with the dogs on top of us!" I added. "Let's go get the Wonder Dogs so we can start practicing!"

It was the last-but-not-least piece of our *very fantastic plan*!

9

EENY, MEENY, MINY, UH-OH!

We walked together to Stefano Wondrous's tent. The three Wonder Dogs are brothers. Stefano dresses them in their own *unique* colors, because he says dogs like to be fancy sometimes, too. *Eeny* wears a red collar. *Meeny* wears a blue one. And *Miny*'s collar is green. All three dogs started barking loud-loud-loud when they saw us coming. They were so happy to see us!

(Dogs are the friendliest!)

But there was one tiny problem with our plan: Stefano was nowhere in sight!

"Can we take the dogs without asking Stefano?" Stella asked.

"Don't worry," Fernando said. "Stefano lets me take them all the time. I help walk them when he's busy."

"Hooray!" I said.

Fact: Having a gooberhead doing teamwork with us was turning out to be very handy!

Fernando opened the dogs' cage and clipped their leashes on one at a time: red for Eeny, blue for Meeny, and green for Miny (of course). I reached into the can of dog treats outside their cage and grabbed a whole bunch.

"Be good dogs and follow us quietly," I told them, waving the treats, "and you can have some snacks!" The dogs wagged their tails all over the place when they saw the snacks.

(Everyone loves snacks.)

Thank goodness gracious we didn't run into any other Sweet Potatoes on the way back to the field behind Fernando's tent. We had my small trampoline and some other props so we could practice putting our new act together. It was complicated, but I wasn't too-too worried. (The Wonder Dogs are very fast learners!)

Zip! I flipped from Clementine's back onto my trampoline. *Bo-iing!*

The dogs were balanced, one on each of Stella's arms and one on her head.

Zap! They jumped, one at a time, from Stella to me!

Zoom! The dogs *leaped* from me on my trampoline up-up-up to Fernando. Now they were on *his* arms and head!

Flip! Stella did her backflip right on Clementine's back!

Flop! I did my backflip on my springy-sproingy trampoline!

Gently, Clementine picked me up with her trunk and placed me onto her back again, behind Stella.

We did it! *We did it!* Now it was time for Fernando to stilt-walk over to us.

"One, two, three, *hup!*" I shouted, like I was Ringmaster Riley, in charge of everything.

But then! I heard it:

A bumblebee.

It was very loud and very buzzish. I wanted to shoo it away. But if I waved my hands, I might lose my balance.

The bee buzzed along, away from me. And right over Fernando's head, into Miny the dog!

Miny started yapping like crazy. And *then* he went totally and completely coconuts!

"Oh no!" Fernando shouted.

Everything was happening lightning-quick. One minute, Fernando, Stella, and I were balancing away. The next minute, the stilts were swaying all over the place, and the dogs were all three barking the loudest of ever.

Fernando began to tilt.

And I knew, right then, in my deepest, darkest heart:

*He was totally going to fall—*kaboom!*—over!*

✻ 10 ✻

SUPERHERO STRONG!

Wobble-wobble-wobble went Fernando's stilts.

Yap-yap-yap went the Wonder Dogs.

Eek! Ack! Oh! went my brain.

I shut my eyes.

I waited for the *kaboom*.

But then:

VROOOM!

ZOOM!

SWOOP!

I peeled my eyes open one by one. Fernando wasn't wobbling anymore. The bumblebee was gone. What was going on?

"Jed!" Stella shouted. "You're stronger than a super-hero!" She was looking down below.

"Jed?" I asked. I looked over, too.

Below Fernando's legs, a Jed-ish head peeped up at me. It *was* Jed, holding on tight-tight-tight to the stilts. Fernando was steady again!

"Holy trapeze!" I shouted. "You saved him!"

"I guess I did," Jed said. He stepped away from Fernando very carefully. "You were just about to crash-land. I heard the barking and came to see what was going on."

"I'll say you did!" Fernando exclaimed. "You dirt-biked around us in a circle like a race-car driver!"

Jed's face went blushy. "I know a few tricks on my bike. But what are you guys doing out here, anyway?"

It was time to be honest. "We were trying to come up with a stupendous new act," I explained. "I know you wanted us to calm down. But we have to try to save the circus!"

Jed made a thoughtful face, but he didn't say anything.

"Fernando, Stella, and I brainstormed some new, on-our-own tricks. But those didn't work out so well. Then we put our heads together to come up with a *teamwork* act. We thought we'd be stronger together, like in that math problem. But we didn't count on bumblebees."

"People usually don't count on bumblebees," Jed agreed.

"That balancing act was our last hope," Stella said. "But we need more practice!"

Jed's forehead wrinkled. "You're still worried about ticket sales? I told you in class, I'm sure you just heard wrong. There's nothing to worry about."

"When grown-ups whisper, there's a *lot* to worry about," I insisted.

"And grown-ups never believe that kids can help!" Stella said.

"That's the truth," I said. "Lady Edwina doesn't even let us trim ribbons for Clara Bear's costumes! She says the sewing scissors are too-too sharp. *Pfft.*"

"Okay," Jed said. "There's one easy way to settle this once and for all. Let's go talk to Ringmaster Riley."

Fernando thought about that for a minute. "Okay," he decided. "My dad will tell me the truth, for sure."

But before Fernando could climb down off his stilts, Miny leaped from the top of Jed's head onto the dirt bike handlebars. The Wonder Dog just sat there, wagging his tail all over. It was so, so funny! Eeny and Meeny followed. They looked extremely proud of their jumping.

We all laughed. Those dogs really were wondrous!

And even with the bumblebee *uh-oh,* Stella, Fernando, and I really *were* very good at balancing.

It didn't matter that we needed more practice. Because looking at Jed with his dirt bike and the balancing dogs, I had an idea.

"Louise?" Stella called to me. "Are you coming? We're going to talk to Ringmaster Riley."

I nodded. "Okay!" I said. Because I had something to tell Ringmaster Riley. There was maybe *another* stupendous way to save the Sweet Potatoes.

And this could be my best *eureka!* idea yet!

11

THE MOST SUPERB-EST PLAN

We found Ringmaster Riley in the Big Top tent. He and Mama and Daddy were deciding where to set up the flying trapeze for the night. The minute we saw the Ringmaster, Fernando and Stella and I ran right up to him, talking all at the same time.

"You need to listen to us!" Fernando shouted.

"Kids can help bring ticket sales *up!*" Stella cried.

Yap! Yip! Yap! barked the Wonder Dogs.

"Okay, okay." Ringmaster Riley laughed. "What's going on?"

"The cotton candy machine exploded! And then Louise heard the grown-ups talking," Fernando explained. "About ticket sales being down."

"And we had a *superb* idea for saving the whole entire circus!" Stella chimed in. "If we could just come up with a stupendous new act!"

"But no one listens to kids," Jed said, giving Mama, Daddy, and the Ringmaster a *glance.*

"Louise, I *did* listen to you," Mama reminded me. "We talked about this the other day."

"I know," I said. "But my squeezy stomach didn't go away."

Ringmaster Riley put his finger on his chin in a thinking way. "Tell me more, Louise."

"We all three heard you arguing with Ethel Teitelbaum! And we saw the cotton candy machine explode," I said, pointing to Fernando and Stella. "Then I heard Chuck Cluck talking to Cady the Bearded Lady. She said ticket sales are down. And that made me worried. Stella was worried, too. And even Ferret-breath—I mean, *Fernando*—thought we should try to save the day."

Daddy laughed. "Cooperation. That's a nice change."

"So we *brainstormed* to try to come up with a new act for each of us. But that didn't work so well. And then we put our heads together to come up with one *teamwork* act we could all do. And that didn't work, either! Fernando's stilts almost went crashing down!"

"Yikes!" Mama said. "Are you all okay?"

"We are!" I said. "Because of *one stupendous person*! So I have a brand-new, brilliant idea for saving the circus."

Stella and Fernando looked confused. Mama, Daddy, and Ringmaster Riley looked curious. I spread my arms out wide like Ringmaster Riley when he was announcing right in the middle of the Big Top ring.

"Presenting . . . the Dirt Bike Daredevil, Jed!" I shouted.

Jed's mouth dropped open. "What?"

Stella clapped her hands and Fernando whistled, excited. "Louise, that's *perfect*!" Stella said.

Ringmaster Riley's eyes twinkled. "Go on," he said.

"Jed is totally, completely, one hundred percent fearless on his dirt bike," I explained. "He could for definitely have his own act. When Fernando's stilts went wobble-ish, Jed zoomed up on his dirt bike like a superhero! He did a loop-de-loop around us, then steadied Fernando easy-peasy! Can you *even*?"

Mama's mouth twitched up in a smile. "I definitely cannot."

"It's the truth," I told her. "Even if *you* aren't worried about ticket sales, I still think our circus could use a daredevil dirt biker! That would be a *showstopper*."*

* SHOWSTOPPER: an AMAZING act that makes the whole audience OOH and AAH!

Ringmaster Riley put his hands on his hips. "It's not a bad idea," he said. He looked at Jed. "What do you think?"

Jed shrugged. "I don't know," he answered. "I'm a teacher. I never thought I'd be a circus performer. Honestly, the idea makes me a little nervous."

I knew how he felt. I was nervous the first time I had to fly on the grown-up trapeze. But now I knew just how to make the nervous feelings go away.

"We'll help you!" I told Jed. "All of us will practice right by your side with you until you're ready for your *fabulous debut!*"

Now Jed smiled. "It probably *would* be fun to show off some of my dirt bike skills. But what about the act you three were working on?"

"That act needs more practice, too," I said. "We can work on our tricks together. After all, you're the one who taught us that problems are easier to solve with *teamwork*."

I felt maple-syrup warm in my stomach now. There was more than one way to save the whole entire circus. Cooperation and sharing the spotlight with Jed could be the very bestest thing for the Sweet Potatoes!

"We did it!" I said. "We saved the day!" I turned back to the grown-ups. "Now let us show you how!"

"Not so fast, Louise," Mama said. "First of all, you shouldn't have jumped to conclusions when you saw Ringmaster Riley argue with Ethel. Sometimes adults argue! That doesn't mean there's a huge problem brewing."

I swallowed. "Okay."

"Now before you show us your act," Riley said, "I

think we should talk to Chuck Cluck and Cady. I'd like you to understand what you overheard."

I looked at Stella. I looked at Fernando. Both of them nodded at me.

I turned back to Ringmaster Riley. "Okay," I said. But my stomach gave one last squeeze.

I was finally going to learn the truth of the whispery things!

12

THE WHOLE ENTIRE TRUTH

It was easy to find Cady the Bearded Lady and Chuck Cluck. They were together, right next to the juggling chickens' coop. The chickens were juggling, and Chuck and Cady were watching close-close-close.

FACT: The chickens were juggling extra-super quickly. Just like everyone was doing everything all of a sudden! Why was the whole entire circus in fast-forward?

"Cady," Ringmaster Riley said, "Louise overheard something the other day. She's a little confused."

"And worried!" I added.

"Maybe I can clear things up," Cady said. "What did you hear, Louise?"

"The other night, after my Tightwire Tango, you were talking to Chuck Cluck. You were saying that ticket sales are *down*. And then I heard you talk about saving the performance!"

Cady looked at Chuck. Chuck looked at Cady. They both looked at Ringmaster Riley.

And then! They *laughed*!

"Louise, you heard completely wrong," Cady said. "What I said to Chuck was that ticket sales are *sound*. *Sound* means *strong*. We're selling lots of tickets! The circus is doing better than ever!"

Better than ever? That was the opposite of needing-to-be-saved! I was so confused. "But then, why did you say we needed to save the performance?"

"*Shave*. I said we needed to *shave some time* off our performance. That means make some of the acts a little shorter. So many people want to come to the show, we're trying to add a second performance to each night!" Cady grinned. "*Two* performances! Twice the audience!"

"Holy trapeze!" I shouted. "That's stupendous!"

FACT: Twice the audience means twice the curtain calls !!! That's twice the clapping parts !! And I Love-love-**LOVE** the clapping parts!!!

TICKETS

12 pm SHOW SOLD OUT!

NEW SHOW ADDED!

NEW

5pm SHOW Tickets Available

5pm Show!

A thought popped into my brain. "But wait!" I said. "Is *that* the reason everyone's been acting so lickety-split quick lately?"

"They have?" Chuck asked. "We thought it was just the juggling chickens."

"They definitely have!" I said. "Tolstoy the Clown was juggling fast-fast-fast, too. And El Fuego Mateo was swallowing fire like fast-forward!"

Now *everyone* laughed!

"It sounds like *all* the Sweet Potatoes had some ideas about saving the circus," Mama said.

Ringmaster Riley stepped forward. "And wait till you hear what these three came up with," he said to Cady and Chuck. "I think we've got a great new act that our double-sized audience will love."

"We do!" I shouted. I gave Stella a BFF squeeze. "We did it!"

"But we *didn't* save the day," Stella said. "Because *actually,* the day didn't need to be saved!"

"Maybe not," I replied. I wrinkled my nose. Stella had a good point.

"You tried, though," Mama said. She made a look-at-the-bright-side face. "And you've got a great new act for our new-and-improved, double-feature show!"

"And isn't it better that the circus didn't need saving?" Daddy added.

I had to smile at that. "You have a point," I said.

"Everything turned out a-okay," Stella said. "And now . . . the show must go on!"

I laughed like craziness. "Better than that!" I said. "Not 'show,' *shows*!"

Two performances! Two times the new act! And *twice* the clapping!

That was an a-okay ending after all!

About the Author

MICOL OSTOW can totally save the day, once she's had her coffee. She lives and works in Brooklyn, New York, where she reads books and tries her hardest to be a real live grown-up. (Sometimes it even works!) Micol is the author of numerous acclaimed books for young adults and children, but Louise Trapeze is her first chapter book series. Learn more about Micol and Louise at micolostow.com.

About the Illustrator

BRIGETTE BARRAGER is an artist, illustrator, designer, and writer of children's books. She recently illustrated the *New York Times* bestseller *Uni the Unicorn* by Amy Krouse Rosenthal. Brigette resides in Los Angeles with her handsome husband, cute doggy, and terrible cat. Visit her at brigetteb.com.

New friends. New adventures.
Find a new series . . . just for you!

FOR THE SPORTS FAN

FOR THE ADVENTURER

FOR THE SUPERSTAR

FOR THE DREAMER

FOR THE ANIMAL LOVER

FOR THE EXPLORER